Katharine Tynan

A Lover's Breast-Knot

Katharine Tynan

A Lover's Breast-Knot

ISBN/EAN: 9783743383913

Manufactured in Europe, USA, Canada, Australia, Japa

Cover: Foto ©Andreas Hilbeck / pixelio.de

Manufactured and distributed by brebook publishing software
(www.brebook.com)

Katharine Tynan

A Lover's Breast-Knot

A LOVER'S BREAST-KNOT

BY

KATHARINE TYNAN
(Mrs Hinkson)

LONDON
ELKIN MATHEWS
1896

CONTENTS

Of this Edition 500 *copies have been printed*

TO HARRY

HEARTSEASE

Heartsease you gave me, richer, rarer
     Than any heartsease blowing, growing.
Not Death shall make me less the wearer
     Of the dear heartsease of your sowing.

Heartsease you gave me for a token
     You took my share of pain and grieving.
A charmed heart to bear unbroken
     Amid Love's sorrow, Love's bereaving.

Heartsease for yesterday, to-morrow,
     And for the dying year and vernal:
To make me flowers the winter thorough,
     For mortal Time and Time eternal.

Take for your heartsease purple, golden.
     Heartsease that bloomed in Love's gold weather,
For all in which I am beholden,
     My heartsease and my heart together!

Love's Trouble

FOR you I fear the stabbing rain,
   The wounding wind;
O wandering love, return again,
   Turn and be kind.
The distant thunder in the hills
   I fear for you;
I fear the lightning's spear that kills,
   Wavering, blue.

For you the noonday sun I dread.
   O noonday sun,
Rest quietly on his dear head,
   My dearest one!
For you all evil beasts I fear,
   All foul affrights
With wingèd shadows that creep anear
   In lonely nights.

Dear angels, guard him where he goes,
   In day and dark;
Lest nigh his path, in lily and rose,
   The serpent lurk.

O, sleepless eyes of blessed ones,
  Watch o'er my love;
And wings that shame th' eternal suns
  Winnow above!

Greater Love

THERE is but one sweet Love, one Love
    unroving,
  Truer than mine may be;
One constant Love beyond all mortal loving,
  Greater than yours for me.

Therefore unto that Love I do commend you,
  So that when mine shall fail
That Love unfailing may wrap round, befriend you,
  That sea of Love prevail.

So that when my poor love is but remembered
  As some sweet thing foregone,
That Love may fill you full with sweets unnumbered,
  And leave you not alone.

O Love eternal, Love supernal, keep him
  If haply I should go ;
In all Love's raptures, Love's rewardings steep him,
  Yea, pay him all I owe !

3   B—3

Love's Bird

WHEN thrushes rest the weary head,
    And linnets lie in gold and green,
When blackbirds on a downy bed
    Are silvered with a moony sheen,

What voice awakes the emerald house?
    What love incarnate flies on wings?
What passion shakes the trembling boughs?
    It is the Bird of Love that sings.

It is the Bird of Love that sings, ·
    Stabbing our silence like a sword,
And Love himself that flies on wings.
    God and enchanter and no bird.

Our moon of honey, our marriage moon
    Rides in the heaven for our delight.
The silver world grows golden soon,
    Honey and gold spilled in the night.

The Bird of Love, the Bird of pain,
    He sings our marriage moon away;
Filling the night with golden rain,
    Betwixt the darkness and the day.

Closer and closer, hold me close,
    For is it Love or Death he sings?
And is it Love or Death that goes
    Through the sweet night with rustling wings?

Love's Flight

THERE is a love of earth, Love,
  A love that flies on wings;
The one hath lowliest birth, Love,
  The other blood of kings.

O look, look, my Sweetheart,
  Where yon skylark flies;
So light and bright, my Sweetheart,
  In the clear skies!

He is our love on wings, Love,
  That flies in sure bliss
Beyond the wreck of things, Love,
  On earth where death is.

And yet not all of heaven:
  He flies back to earth
To find his heaven at even
  Beside his own hearth.

O look, look, my own Love,
  'Tis our love on wings!
But, ah, the wingless love, Love,
  'Mid earth's creeping things.

Love's Watchfulness

WHEN you awake I wake,
  And when you sleep I sleep.
Your lightest sigh will break
  My sweetest dreams and deep.

My heart watches aware
  Whether I wake or sleep.
Though far in dreams I fare,
  Call, and my heart will leap.

The grave is not so low,
  The way to Heaven so steep,
But I should surely know
  If my Love stirred in sleep.

What world, what starry sphere
  My heart in dreams could keep,
If you wanted me, dear,
  If you should wake and weep?

Love's Garden

A LITTLE garden, great enough
    To hold Love's wings.
Yea, and the sacred Bird of Love,
    Hark, how he sings!

The ardent Flower of Love, likewise,
    Burns in the brake.
Love's wings are set with myriad eyes,
    Ever awake.

Heavy with honey flies the bee
    From rose to rose ;
Powdered with gold dust to the knee,
    He comes and goes.

The secret song the nightingale
    Sang to the moon,
It shall be hidden by Love's veil,
    Now it is noon.

The secret thing the golden bee
    Said to the rose,
Though it be known to thee and me,
    Shall we disclose?

8

Ah no ! Love's secrets let us keep,
    Lest the winged god
Angered, go seeking, while we sleep,
    Some new abode.

Love Inconstant

AFTER April month and May
    Love of birds will fly away.
After June light loves grown chilly
Part, though tarry rose and lily.
O alas! such loves should sunder,
They who made the world a wonder,
Raining from their honey throats
Golden notes and silver notes!

O in April what unrest
Stirs the swallow's sea-born breast
For some love of old and golden,
Where pale orchards bloom unfolden!
For some silent heartstring stirred,
Some lost heaven remembered.
And the old dream calls him home,
Home by trackless skies and foam.

O alas, such things should be!
Cold as stone are he and she:
Empty gapes the nest and wide
They two planned with such sweet pride.

The sweet nestlings flown as far
As the light-winged lost loves are.
Love, whose love endures, see then
How sweet Love is wronged again!

How these birds, from lark to sparrow,
Snap his bow and blunt his arrow!

Love in Absence

I

LOVE IMPATIENT

COME while the sweet Spring stays, O come!
  Come ere the nightingale be dumb;
While on her eggs his mate doth sit,
And all the chestnut lamps are lit.

Come, ere the baby leaves grow old.
Crumpled and soft, these keep the fold
Of tight enswathèd buds, O come!
While yet the swallow is new to home.

Come while our orchard like a bride
Blushes through white, and evening-tide
Hangs all the pear tree with such white,
Spun from the moon-rays for delight.

Come while the yellow moon still shows,
A moon of honey, a golden rose.
And while all night in rapt content
Our garden of Eden spills its scent.

Come, ere the cuckoo's song is over,
Come in the day of every lover,
When every lover still wings for home;
Come, ere the nightingale be dumb.

.

II

I WOULD not shorten if I might
   By one sweet hour the hours that stand
Betwixt me and my heart's delight.

May and the lilac in the land,
   All rapturous sounds, and scents at night,
The days spill out their golden sand.

Sweet is the garden, white with bloom,
   Heavy with honey, drenched with scent,
Wherein a bride awaits her groom,

In a most measureless content.
   With gold and white day fills the loom,
And soon the moon-gold nights are spent.

I would not shorten by an hour
   The hours wherein I wait for you
With Love and all the world in flower.

So sweet, so sweet in sun and dew,
   It is the hour of Love's full power,
Yet come, and make my world anew!

Home-Coming

O PASSIONATE pilgrim, was the way
  So long then, was the day so long
From the blue matin till 'twas gray?
  From morning till the evening-song?

Was it so long, love, while you came
  Nearer each minute? lead-foot, slow,
Did the day round to evening-flame?
  And was the daylight slow to go?

And did your eager eyes look far
  To see the crescent moon rise bright?
And Hesper, your home-coming star,
  Did Hesper tarry long that night?

At last the moon rained gold, and lest
  The moon-gold were too cold, there fell
Drifting of bloom about your nest;
  That night the nightingale sang well.

O sweet day full of scent and song,
  Sweetly it wore from dawn to even;
And yet the sweet day did us wrong,
  Since evening brought the lover's heaven.

15

The Lark in Love

THE lark that's climbing stair on stair
   His ladder of light that swings in air,
Hath a new note for every rung,
The lark's in love and young.

But soon the clouds allure no more,
No more the silver-damasked floor;
In spirals was his outward track,
But headlong comes he back.

He falls, shot through the burning heart,
Yea, through the heart by Love's own dart;
Too well the·cunning archer knew
The arrow he sent was true.

But, lark, what wisdom dost thou prove
Whose wings, still tethered by thy love,
Carry thy song to Paradise,
Yet sweeter are her eyes.

That was her praise, thy song that poured,
And his of wedded lovers, the lord.
Io Hymen! Thou happy boy,
Drunken with love and joy.

Io Hymen! O, speckled breast,
Minstrel of thine own wedding feast,
Lover and bridegroom, singing still,
How Love shall have his will !

Love's Carefulness

UNTO myself I am grown dear,
    Being dear to you,
And fearful with a double fear
    In all I do,
Lest that some evil chance should prove
Ruin of that poor thing you love.

O this woman will love her girl
    And that her boy !
I keep not even the golden curl
    Of our dead joy ;
Now both my loves in one are given
Ever to you who make my heaven.

If all our palaces were dust
    Blown on the wind,
I might some other woman trust
    To be as kind,
To love as well as I—but then
What love could bid you love again ?

O generous giver, who hast given
        Once and for aye,
For life and death, for earth and heaven,
        As for to-day,
I love myself because you hold
Every hair of my head as gold.

Love's Summer

I

CALLING THE BIRDS

WHO close beside our window pane,
  Whistles thrice at the dawn of day,
And listens for his answer fain?
      Toujours gai.

Who bids the merry din resound,
  While oaten pipes are silvery gray,
Ere chanticleer first turns him round?
      Toujours gai.

Who bids the corncrake, shrill and blithe,
  Wake up on his sweet couch of hay,
And whirr against the mower's scythe?
      Toujours gai.

Who hales the finch from dreams of love,
  And linnet to his roundelay,
And from Love's arms the wooing dove?
      Toujours gai.

Who calls the robin and the starling,
   And bids the blackbird's flute to play,
The thrush to sing : O darling, darling?
                  Toujours gai.

Who is it wakes the sparrows' wall,
   And sets a-tremble every spray,
With flutter, and chatter, and trill, and call?
                  Toujours gai.

This whistling thing at sweet o' the year,
   O is he bird, or boy, or fay?
Mayhap, some fairy chanticleer.
                  Toujours gai.

May he be fed on honey and kisses,
   And where the undying roses stay,
Wake the sweet world to newer blisses.
                  Toujours gai.

SUMMER-SWEET

HONEY-SWEET, sweet as honey smell the
    lilies,
  Little lilies of the gold in a ring;
Little censers of pale gold are the lilies,
  That the wind, sweet and sunny, sets a-swing.

Smell the rose, sweet of sweets, all a-blowing!
  Hear the cuckoo call in dreams, low and sweet!
Like a very John-a-Dreams coming, going.
  There's honey in the grass at our feet.

There's honey in the leaf and the blossom,
  And honey in the night and the day.
And honey-sweet the heart in Love's bosom,
  And honey-sweet the words Love will say.

III

BEES in the white and scarlet cell
   Of bean-flowers and in beds of thyme;
The leader of the sheep his bell
   Ringeth my even-song and prime;
He leads his flock at morning early
   Out to the dark grass sewn with gold,
And when the evening dews are pearly,
   Back to the fold.

Somewhere they mow the grass: the sound
   Brings with it fresh and fragrant breaths.
And little airs all scent be-drowned,
   Blown from the white and purple heaths.
The last bird sings his waning passion.
   And you, whose love can never fail,
Take up the burden and narration
   Of the sweet tale.

IV

AUGUST WEATHER

DEAD heat and windless air,
   And silence over all;
Never a leaf astir,
   But the ripe apples fall;
Plums are purple-red,
   Pears amber and brown;
Thud! in the garden-bed
   Ripe apples fall down.

Air like a cider-press
   With the bruised apples' scent;
Low whistles express
   Some sleepy bird's content;
Still world and windless sky,
   A mist of heat o'er all;
Peace like a lullaby,
   And the ripe apples fall.

Love's Praises

LET other ladies name their loves
    With flushing cheek and bashful eye,
And voices as the gentle dove's,
    Crooning her love-song like a sigh;
I know not such sweet ways, in faith,
And yet I love my Love till death.

When I would tell how he excels
    All other men my eyes grow dim,
My heart shakes and my bosom swells,
    And only tears I have for him.
To my own heart with tears I say
His name, and silent turn away.

Let other ladies sit and sun
    Like turtle-doves their shining heads,
And tell their lovers every one,
    Their kindness and their gentle deeds.
How this is brave and that is true.
Only my tears are praise for you.

O secrets we may not impart,
    Being too tender to be told;
And sweetnesses that break the heart,
    Too great for one poor heart to hold.
Silence and tears beseem them best,
And hidden eyes in my Love's breast.

Love's House

O in Love's emerald house
    Of emerald chestnut boughs,
  The brown wife broods upon blue eggs and dear,
Nor finds the gold days long
Hearing her true Love's song
  Of love and wedding in the sweet o' the year.

And in Love's golden house
Of golden chestnut boughs,
  The brown bird to his sweet sings wild and clear;
Though little ones are gone,
The true Love lingers on,
  For two old lovers in the fall o' the year.

Annus Mirabilis

(1893)

THE year that brought our hearts' desire,
   The Spring came with a sudden glow ;
     No tender Spring that shyly comes
     With primroses and apple-blooms,
But garbed as with a golden fire
   Of her own daffodills a-blow.

O year beyond all years that were !
   The Summer followed fast in May ;
     Scarce had the nightingales begun
     When the red rose out-burned the sun,
And scent of ripe fruit in the air
   Mixed with the honey-breath of hay.

That year the Spring came over again,
   There were two Summers in that year.
     In August there were bird-nestings
     And second broods and such sweet things,
And on the world a golden rain,
   And a new blossom on the pear.

That year the year was always May.
  Our year in whose sweet close shall come
    No winter with a waning sky,
    Nor sad leaves fall, nor roses die;
But roses, roses all the way,
  And never a nightingale be dumb.

Love at Easter

SING *to the Lord a new song !*
　Because the Spring comes newly,
And every slender sapling
　Has budded green and red.
Sing to the Lord a new song !
　The skylark sings it truly,
Since all in dewy April
　His love and he are wed.

Sing to the Lord a new song !
　For every bird's a lover,
And o'er the purple furrows
　The green spears nod and wave.
Sing to the Lord a new song !
　Since Lenten fasts are over,
And Easter's gone in glory,
　And Christ has left the grave.

Sing to the Lord a new song !
　A song of love and wedding,
For every bird is building
　His nest in bower and tree.
Sing to the Lord a new song !
　The tufts of soft wool spreading
Where a brown wife and babies
　This April-tide shall be.

Of the True Marriage

UNTO His servant on a day
  The Lord revealed His hidden way.

He said: "Within this city great,
  Where sin still slays the Lamb of God,
What dost thou think I contemplate
  For comfort when I look abroad?"
His servant answered: "Yonder church
Crowded at Mass-time to the porch."

The Lord replied: "Not so"; and then,
  His servant guessed to make Him glad
The priest where he sat shriving men;
  The wounded healed; the orphan clad;
The widow's tears wiped off; the poor
Fed from another's little store.

And then he guessed the saint who died
  Last night; Fra Leo, vigil-pale,
Painting the wings of Heaven; Christ's bride
  New-wed, beneath her shadowy veil;
The grey cross in the market-place
With children playing at its base.

31

And many things of earth and heaven:
    The Convent garden and the doves;
The Western sky aflame at even;
    The mountains and the orange groves;
The sea that moaned alway and prayed:
And yet the Lord God shook His head.

He said: "Lo, in thy city I see
    A wife and husband, full of love,
Whose lives in loving harmony
    Are set all death and change above.
I see: and leaning from my place,
I bless them in their hidden grace.

Whose love and peace and sweet accord
Comfort Me greatly": said the Lord.

TO GODFREY

LOVE-LIES-BLEEDING

His small hands brought a flower for me,
    A flower of love and sorrow.
Now angels over the gray sea
    Bid my sweetheart good-morrow.

His face was sweeter than a rose,—
    But O Love's rose is thorny!
He nestled in my breast so close
    Before he went his journey.

O days when he and I lay there,
    O he and I together,—
All in a trance of peace and prayer
    In the rich August weather.

I gather from the self-same root
    My flower of Love lies bleeding.
Ah, Love, one wound from head to foot,
    Past help and interceding!

D—2

.

Love Comfortless

THE child is in the night and rain
   On whom no tenderest wind might blow,
And out alone in a hurricane.
                   Ah, no,
The child is safe in Paradise!

The snow is on his gentle head,
   His little feet are in the snow,
O, very cold is his small bed!
                   Ah, no,
Lift up your heart, lift up your eyes!

Over the fields and out of sight,
   Beside the lonely river's flow,
Lieth the child this bitter night.
                   Ah, no,
The child sleeps under Mary's eyes!

What wandering lamb cries sore distressed,
   Whilst I with fire and comfort go?
O, let me warm him in my breast!
                   Ah, no,
'Tis warm in God's lit nurseries!

The Sheepfold

THE Shepherd of the sheepfold leant
    Upon his crook, and saw within
The fold his milky ewes content,
    His white lambs innocent of sin.

The milky mothers giving suck
    He saw, and merry lambs at play,
Yet, leaning on his shepherd's crook,
    His eyes, his heart, were turned away.

His tender thoughts were turned apart
    To where his orphaned lambs cried on ;
Their cries lay heavy on his heart—
    Poor milkless lambkins and undone.

With tears he saw the milky dams
    Go dropping milk upon the grass;
These were the mothers of dead lambs,
    The mothers of dead lambs, alas !

O little lambs that would not live,
    Your milk runs all to bitter waste,
Your milk that makes the Shepherd grieve,
    Runs out like tears so hot and fast.

O comfort, comfort then those sheep,
  Whose little lovely lambs are dead.
The milk that makes the Shepherd weep
  Runs out like tears, and none is fed.

Holy Innocents

GOLD on gold, snow on snow,
    Height on height, row on row;
Greater in number these
Than the sands of the seas.

Yea, past all counting far,
Flower on flower, star on star,
Dimpled shoulder, cheek of peach,
As they lean each to each.

Golden heads, brows of pearl,
O many a boy and girl,
O many a girl and boy,
Mother's grief, mother's joy.

But amid snow and gold,
Gathered warm from the cold,
Fairer than gold or snow,
Should be two that I know.

Love's Thanksgiving

O how good God is that He sends
    Stores of unfailing love to me,
And work and prayer and praise of friends,
    Blackbirds and thrushes in the tree,
And sheep bells in the fields, and roses
    And all the sweets of May and June,
And lavender and dew and posies,
        And sun and moon.

O how good God is that He sends
    Bean-rows in blossom, bees i' the hive,
Gray dawn and golden evening-ends,
    And a glad heart to be alive;
A grateful mind and quiet fancies,
    Shade from the sun, and sleep at night,
And clumps of brown and golden pansies,
        And lilies white.

O how good God is that He sends
    A little child to be all ours,
Mine and my dearest Love's, and tends
    Our blossom in the sun and showers,

And bids His angels still keep near him
   Lest that the little feet should miss,
And wings of angels still to bear him
       Ever in bliss.

     *   *   *   *

O how good God is that He keeps
   The child for ever and ever well,
Above the tempests and the deeps,
   In joy no tongue can tell.
Our little lamb of God goes straying,
   By daisied meadows, 'neath dappled skies;
Our little lamb of God goes playing
       Under God's eyes.

Love's Winter

O IF the shortest day were past,
    Or if it were the shortest day,
'Twere easier to take heart at last
    To face the outward way.

O if above a darling head
    The snowdrops danced in the wind's play,
Then joy might steal in sorrow's tread
    To meet the hope of May.

But now the shortest day is gone,
    The year of sorrow gone for aye.
Ho, traveller, turn and face the sun,
    For night gives place to day.

Ho, traveller, take the outward track,
    Lift up your heart, give thanks, and pray.
God knows some New Year brings you back
    What Old Year took away.

Love's Rose

M Y rose shall have no care at all,
　　While the years rise and the years fall,
Shall keep its gold heart folded close
In the warm petals of my rose.

Winds that deflower may rave at will
Round the June rose to work her ill—
Scatter her leaves of pearl and peach,
O, but my rose is out of reach.

In the shut bud the canker-worm
Steals to defile her and deform.
Near my one rose no ill shall creep,
Seeing his plot kind angels keep.

The wind that swings him low and high
Softer is than a lullaby:
The wind that swings him high and low
Goes as his cradle used to go.

Winter shall never find my Sweet,
Nor shall he faint in summer heat,
Filled full of dews and bathed in sun,
Happy he is, my tender one.

God is his gardener, so 'tis plain,
God's rose shall never fret again,
Never be sad, never be gray,
Blooming a bud for ever and aye.

Yea, my sweet rose God's eyes shall please;
O, what a happy lot is his!
Blessed the will that doth accord
Me to grow roses for my Lord.

Garden Secrets

A GARDEN in the Summer,
   Wherein the birds and I
Built nests for some new-comer
   To swing against the sky.

Garden of rose and lily,
   And dream of dew and scent,
Where never a wind was chilly,
   And hearts were well content.

The day smoked like a censer
   Till evening brought the shade,
And leaves grew thicker, denser,
   And we were not afraid.

Ah, birds, so blithe and cheerful,
   We guessed not how should come
The Autumn gray and tearful,
   The Winter cold and dumb.

Ah, building days and brooding!
   We guessed not how 'twould be
With sad rains flooding, flooding,
   Our ruined nests in tree.

The Child in Heaven

THE nursery windows were cold and black,
　　The nursery hearth it was gray and sad;
She moaned for the child that would never come
　　back,
　　Her heart was broken for her little lad.
She had folded his garments and put them away,
　　She had hidden his cradle quite out of sight:
But the child was glad in the light of day,
　　While she was caught in the bitter night.

He thinks of his mother through all that cheer;
He would never forget in a hundred year.

The silence ached for the baby's cry.
　　O silence, silence and loneliness!
And the thought of the empty nursery
　　Cried at her heart with a keen distress—
Knocked at her heart like a ghost of the night,
　　Followed her ever or near or far:
But her little boy he is clad in white,
　　In the land that is over the morning star.

He thinks of his mother through all that cheer;
He would never forget in a hundred year.

His bed was soft as a nest of roses,
　　His robes were all of the linen spun,
He had taken nought but a handful of posies
　　When he went out on his way alone—
When he went out where she might not follow,
　　And left her stricken and cold and bare,
His radiant journey by hill and hollow,
　　To the dear God's House in the glittering air.

He thinks of his mother through all that cheer;
He would never forget in a hundred year.

She will come one day to God's nursery,
　　Where His little babies are safe and warm,
And lift the little one to her knee,
　　And lose the ache of the empty arm,
And lose the ache of the empty heart,
　　And fashion newly Love's empty nest,
And kiss his brows and his lips apart,
　　And give him milk from her lonely breast.

He thinks of his mother through all that cheer;
He would never forget in a hundred year.

Love in Heaven

THE child is rocked on Mary's knees,
    Her lullaby stills his alarms,
Love's cradle gives him happy ease,
    Love's nest of love within her arms:
" Lullaby," she singeth, " Pretty babe of sorrow,
Thy mother comes to stay with thee to-morrow."

One angel hold his basin, one
    His ewer of golden water sweet,
And one his robe to put him on
    And one his pillow and his sheet.
" O mystery," they cry, " of love and sorrow,
Sleep sweet, dear babe, thy mother comes to-
    morrow."

Immortal angels standing by,
    Kiss that sweet babe on Mary's knee.
" Blessed the woman is," they sigh,
    " Whose motherhood hath given her thee.
Happy her lot in mortal joy and sorrow
Who lost thee yesterday but finds to-morrow."

        E

NOTE

Note 1. Page 47.—The refrain of these verses, "The Child in Heaven," belongs to a poem by the late W. B. Rands,—"Matthew Browne." At the time I used it I was not aware of this; but the poem had been built up about it, and afterwards anything else seemed less right.

NEARLY all the verses in this volume have appeared in the *Pall Mall Gazette.* Of the exceptions, three were published in the *Illustrated London News*, one in the *English Illustrated Magazine*, one in the *Sunday Magazine*, one in the *New Review*, one in *Black and White*, and two in the *Irish Monthly*. To the various editors my acknowledgments and thanks.

PRINTED BY R. FOLKARD AND SON, 22, DEVONSHIRE STREET,
QUEEN SQUARE, LONDON, W.C.

Catalogue

of

Publications

FRUCTUS INTER FOLIA

TELEGRAPHIC
ADDRESS—

"ELEGANTIA,
LONDON."

A.J.GASKIN

ELKIN MATHEWS
LONDON VIGO, STRT. W

ALL THE BOOKS IN THIS CATALOGUE ARE
PUBLISHED AT NET PRICES

1896-97

Vigo Viatica

Lector! eme, lege, & gaudebis

List of Books

IN

BELLES LETTRES

(Including some Importations and Transfers)

PUBLISHED BY

ELKIN MATHEWS

VIGO STREET, LONDON, W.

N.B.—The Authors and Publisher reserve the right of reprinting any book in this list, except in cases where a stipulation has been made to the contrary, and of printing a separate edition of any of the books for America. In the case of limited Editions, the numbers mentioned do not include the copies sent for review, nor those supplied to the public libraries. The prices of books not yet published are subject to variation.

The Books mentioned in this Catalogue can be obtained to order by any Bookseller. It should be noted also that they are supplied to the Trade on terms which will not allow of discount.

◆§§◆

The following are a few of the Authors represented in this Catalogue:

ALFRED AUSTIN, P.L.
R. D. BLACKMORE.
ROBERT BRIDGES.
BLISS CARMAN.
E. R. CHAPMAN.
CANON DIXON.
ERNEST DOWSON.
MICHAEL FIELD.
T. GORDON HAKE.
ARTHUR HALLAM.
W. C. HAZLITT.
KATHARINE HINKSON.
HERBERT P. HORNE.
RICHARD HOVEY.
LEIGH HUNT.

SELWYN IMAGE.
LIONEL JOHNSON.
CHARLES LAMB.
P. B. MARSTON.
WILLIAM MORRIS.
HON. RODEN NOEL.
MAY PROBYN.
F. YORK POWELL.
WILLIAM SHARP.
J. A. SYMONDS.
HENRY VAN DYKE.
THEODORE WATTS-DUNTON.
FREDERICK WEDMORE.
P. H. WICKSTEED.
W. B. YEATS.

ABBOTT (DR. C. C.).

TRAVELS IN A TREE-TOP. Sm. 8vo. 5s. net.

Philadelphia: J. B. Lippincott Company.

THE BIRDS ABOUT US   73 Engravings.   Second Edition.
Thick cr. 8vo.   5s. 6d. net.

Philadelphia: J. B. Lippincott Company.

ARMOUR (MARGARET).

THAMES SONNETS AND SEMBLANCES. By Mrs. W. B.
MACDOUGALL (MARGARET ARMOUR). With 12 full-
page Illustrations, Decorated Title-page and Tail-piece
by W. B. MACDOUGALL. Fcap. 4to.   5s. net.
[*In preparation.*

AUSTIN (ALFRED).

LESZKO THE BASTARD: A Tale of Polish Grief. First
Edition (1877). Crown 8vo.   3s. 6d. net.

The few remaining copies (150) of the above book having
been transferred to the advertiser, he begs to call the
attention of book-buyers to the fact that this interesting
Narrative Poem is not to be found in the collected
edition of the Laureate's works.

BATEMAN (MAY).

SONNETS AND SONGS. With a title design by JOHN D.
MACKENZIE. Fcap. 8vo.   3s. 6d. net.

" It is refreshing to find in these days verse so passionate, and at the same time
so little physiological. . . ."—*Times.*

" In form and style, Miss Bateman's Poems, alike in the sonnet sequence and in
the miscellaneous verses, reach a very high standard; nor are they wanting in true
poetical inspiration; while they are instinct with the atmosphere of the country, and
especially of country flowers."—*Queen.*

BINYON (LAURENCE).

LYRIC POEMS, with title page by SELWYN IMAGE. Sq.
16mo.   5s. net.

"This little volume of LYRIC POEMS displays a grace of fancy, a spontaneity
and individuality of inspiration, and a felicitous command of metre and diction, which
lift the writer above the average of the minor singers of our time. . . . We may
expect much from the writer of 'An April Day,' or of the strong concluding lines on
the present age from a piece entitled ' Present and Future.' "—*Times.*

FIRST BOOK OF LONDON VISIONS. (ELKIN MATHEWS'
SHILLING GARLAND). Fcap. 8vo   1s. net.
[*Second Edition.*

" Mr. Binyon leads off in Mr. Elkin Mathews' new poetical series . . .
with a book of new verses, 'London Visions,' and there seems to me to be no
question about the uncommon worth of these. . . . They are twelve genuine

BINYON (LAURENCE).—continued.

things cut out of the heart of London life, and some of them are poems of a big order. . . . The stuff of poetry is in him, as it is in few of our pleasant verse-writers to-day; and I doubt if any of the London poets—I am not forgetting Mr. Henley—has put so much of actual London into his poetry."—*Sketch.*

"A gravity and gentleness of thought and feeling, warm sympathies, and a power of making us see pictures, mark all the twelve poems here. . . . His verse impresses us more than that of many stormier, more brilliant singers. We shall look with eagerness for his Second Book of Visions."—*Bookman.*

"Mr. Elkin Mathews has had many happy ideas from the time he started the little Mecca of Vigo Street, which will figure largely in the future history of literature in the late nineteenth century. One does not remember any better notion than this of shilling volumes of new poetry. . . . Anyone who has even the faintest love of poetry should buy this splendid shillingsworth—a thing of beauty clad in brown paper, decorated as only Mr. Selwyn Image knows how. Apart from the certainty of its being a much sought after volume in coming days, it is genuine true currency, pure gold, loyally and well wrought."—*Bookselling.*

BLACKMORE (R. D.)

    FRINGILLA : OR, SOME TALES IN VERSE. By the Author of "Lorna Doone." With Eleven full-page Illustrations and numerous vignettes and initials by LOUIS FAIRFAX-MUCKLEY and Three by JAMES W. R. LINTON. Crown 4to. 10s. *net.*

"'Fringilla' must be looked upon as Mr. Blackmore's diversions, and as such it is very delightful. A whimsical originality, an imaginative wealth of detail, a pleasant sense of humour are among Mr. Blackmore's qualities as a poet."—*Speaker.*

"Mr. Blackmore's verse is cultured and careful; it is full of knowledge; it has every quality which commands our respect; it has an old-world charm of gentleness and peace."—MR. W. L. COURTNEY, in the *Daily Telegraph.*

"The charming and accomplished drawings of Mr. Fairfax-Muckley, so finely designed, so admirably decorative."—*Academy.*

BOWCHER (HAVERING).

    THE C MAJOR OF LIFE: A Novel. Cr. 8vo. 3s. 6d. *net*

    New York: Frederick A. Stokes Company.

"A RARE NOVEL.

"We commend this volume with an entire sincerity to all lovers of that literature which is quiet, wise, and good. 'The C Major of Life' is a tale of men and women, of love and the flouting of love, of clashing temperaments and contending ambitions. . . . It has delicacy—delicacy is not the note of the modern novel. It creates its own atmosphere, and excites a genuine, if not a breathless, interest. It is written quietly, composedly, yet with force and feeling. When you lay it down—which you are not likely to do until you have finished it—you feel you have spent your time well and wisely, and you have a sense of gratitude to the author. To fling down such a book as this to the great howling herd of novel readers in town and country, who are fed on such food as 'The Sorrows of Satan' or such strange meat as 'Jude the Obscure,' is, we should surmise, a rash venture; but it takes all sorts to make a world, and we are certain that 'The C Major of Life' will give pleasure to thousands, if only the right thousands happen to hear of it and read it."—*Mr. Augustine Birrell,* Q.C., M.P.

[Isham Facsimile Reprint]

BRETON (NICHOLAS).

No WHIPPINGE, NOR TRIPPINGE, BUT A KINDE FRIENDLY SNIPPINGE. London, 1601. A Facsimile Reprint, with the original Borders to every page, with a Bibliographical Note by CHARLES EDMONDS. 200 copies, printed on hand-made paper at the CHISWICK PRESS. 12mo. 3s. 6d. net.

Also 50 copies Large Paper. 5s. net.

Facsimile reprint from the semi-unique copy discovered in the autumn of 1867 by Mr. Charles Edmonds in a disused lumber room at Lamport Hall, Northants (Sir Charles E. Isham's), and purchased lately by the British Museum authorities. When Dr. A. B. Grosart collected Breton's Works a few years ago for his "Chertsey Worthies Library," he was forced to confess that certain of Breton's most coveted books were missing and absolutely unavailable. The semi-unique example under notice was one of these.

BRIDGES (ROBERT).

ODE FOR THE BICENTENARY COMMEMORATION OF HENRY PURCELL, with other Poems, and a Preface on the Musical Setting of Poetry. (ELKIN MATHEWS' SHILLING GARLAND). [Second Edition.

"The 'Ode to Music' has fine passages."—Spectator.
"A poem admirable alike in feeling and expression."—Times.
"The Ode is a fine work and peculiarly happy as being fine in a kind of poetry analogous in its way to the kind of music that Purcell wrote—well ordered, solid stately. . . . One may think of Dryden while reading it."—Scotsman.

BYRON (MAY).

A LITTLE BOOK OF LYRICS. [In preparation.

CARMAN (BLISS).

LOW TIDE ON GRAND PRÉ; a Book of Lyrics. Second Edition. Small 8vo. 3s. 6d. net.

"A charming little book."——Athenæum.

BEHIND THE ARRAS: A BOOK OF THE UNSEEN. With designs by T. B. METEYARD. Fcap. 8vo. 5s. net.

"A strange, restless, decidedly impressive book with a lurid glow about the lyrics it contains. Mr. Carman's vocabulary is rich and exotic. . . . The book contains rich poetical ore. . . . |It is sumptuously printed, and strikingly bound."—Pall Mall Gazette.
"A brilliant and free fancy decorates the fabric of his thoughts, as though the wind should wave the arras and yield us glimpses of undying roses."—Speaker.

CARMAN (BLISS) & RICHARD HOVEY.

SONGS FROM VAGABONDIA. With Decorations by TOM
B. METEYARD. Fcap. 8vo. 5s. net.
Boston : Copeland & Day.

" The Authors of the small joint volume called ' Songs from Vagabondia,' have
an unmistakable right to the name of poet. These little snatches have the spirit of a
gipsy Omar Khayyám. They have always careless verve, and often careless felicity ;
they are masculine and rough, as roving songs should be. . . . Here, certainly,
is the poet's soul. . . . You have the whole spirit of the book in such an unfor-
getable little lyric as ' In the House of Idiedaily.' . . We refer the reader to the
delightful little volume itself, which comes as a welcome interlude amidst the highly
wrought introspective poetry of the day."—FRANCIS THOMPSON, in *Merry England.*

" Bliss Carman is the author of a delightful volume of verse, ' Low Tide on
Grand Pré,' and Richard Hovey is the foremost of the living poets of America, with
the exception, perhaps, of Bret Harte and Joaquim Miller, whose names are more
familiar. He sounds a deeper note than either of these, and deals with loftier
themes."—*Dublin Express.*

" Both possess the power of investing actualities with fancy, and leaving them
none the less actual ; of setting the march music of the vagabond's feet to words ; of
being comrades with nature, yet without presumption. And they have that charm,
rare in writers of verse, of drawing the reader into the fellowship of their own zest
and contentment."—*Athenæum.*

MORE SONGS FROM VAGABONDIA. With decorations by
T. B. METEYARD. Fcap. 8vo. 5s. net.
Boston : Copeland & Day.

CHAPMAN (ELIZABETH RACHEL).

A LITTLE CHILD'S WREATH : A Sonnet Sequence. With
title page and cover designed by SELWYN IMAGE.
Second Edition. Sq. 16mo., green buckram. 3s. 6d. net.
New York: Dodd, Mead & Company.

" Contains many tender and pathetic passages, and some really exquisite and
subtle touches of childhood nature. . . . The average excellence of the sonnets
is undoubted."—*Spectator.*

" While they are brimming with tenderness and tears, they are marked with the
skilled workmanship of the real poet."—*Glasgow Herald.*

" Evidently describes very real and intense sorrow. Its strains of tender sympathy will appeal specially to those whose hearts have been wrung by the loss of
young child, and the verses are touching in their simplicity "—*Morning Post.*

" Re-assures us on its first page by its sanity and its simple tenderness."—*Bookman.*

COLERIDGE (HON. STEPHEN).

THE SANCTITY OF CONFESSION : A Romance. 2nd edition. Printed by CLOWES & SON. 250 copies. Cr. 8vo.
3s. net.   [*Very few remain.*

Mr. GLADSTONE writes :—"I have read the singularly well told story. . . .
It opens up questions both deep and dark ; it cannot be right to accept in religion
or anything else a secret which destroys the life of an innocent fellow creature."

CORBIN (JOHN).

THE ELIZABETHAN HAMLET: A Study of the Sources, and of Shakspere's Environment, to show that the Mad Scenes had a Comic Aspect now Ignored. With a Prefatory Note by F. YORK POWELL, Regius Professor of Modern History at the University of Oxford. Small 4to. 3s. 6d. net.

New York: Charles Scribner's Sons. [*Very few remain.*

DANTE.

LA COMMEDIA DI DANTE. A New Text carefully Revised with the aid of the most recent Editions and Collations. Thick Fcap. 8vo. 4s. 6d. net.

DAVIES (R. R.).

SOME ACCOUNT OF THE OLD CHURCH AT CHELSEA AND OF ITS MONUMENTS. [*In preparation.*

DE GRUCHY (AUGUSTA).

UNDER THE HAWTHORN, AND OTHER VERSES. With Frontispiece by WALTER CRANE. Printed at the RUGBY PRESS. 300 copies. Cr. 8vo. 5s. net.

"Distinguished by the attractive qualities of grace and refinement, and a purity of style that is as refreshing as a limpid stream in the heat of a summer's noon. . . . The charm of these poems lies in their naturalness, which is indeed an admirable quality in song."—*Saturday Review.*

DIXON (CANON R. WATSON).

SONGS AND ODES. (ELKIN MATHEWS' SHILLING GARLAND, No. V.). Fcap. 8vo. 1s. net.

DOWSON (ERNEST).

DILEMMAS: Stories and Studies in Sentiment. (A Case of Conscience.—The Diary of a Successful Man.—An Orchestral Violin.—The Statute of Limitations.—Souvenirs of an Egoist). Crown 8vo. 3s. 6d. net.

New York: Frederick A. Stokes Company.

"Unquestionably they are good stories, with a real human interest in them."—*St. James's Gazette.*

"'A Case of Conscience' . . . an exceedingly good story. At first sight it might appear unfinished, as one of the problems presented is left unsolved; but one soon feels that anything more would have spoilt the art with which the double tragedy of the two men's lives is flashed before the reader in a few pages."—*Athenæum.*

"These stories can be read with pure enjoyment, for along with subtlety of thought and grace of diction there is true refinement."—*Liverpool Mercury.*

FIELD (MICHAEL).

SIGHT AND SONG (Poems on Pictures). Printed by
CONSTABLES. 400 copies. 12mo. 5s. net.
[Very few remain.

STEPHANIA: A TRIALOGUE IN THREE ACTS. Frontispiece, colophon, and ornament for binding designed
by SELWYN IMAGE. Printed by FOLKARD & SON.
250 copies (200 for sale). Pott 4to. 6s. net.
[Very few remain.

"We have true drama in 'Stephania.' . . . . Stephania, Otho, and
Sylvester II., the three persons of the play, are more than mere names. . . . .
Besides great effort, commendable effort, there is real greatness in this play; and the
blank verse is often sinewy and strong with thought and passion."—*Speaker.*

"'Stephania' is striking in design and powerful in execution. It is a highly
dramatic 'trialogue' between the Emperor Otho III., his tutor Gerbert, and Stephania,
the widow of the murdered Roman Consul, Crescentius. The poem contains much
fine work, and is picturesque and of poetical accent. . . ."—*Westminster Review.*

A QUESTION OF MEMORY: A PLAY IN FOUR ACTS.
100 copies only. 8vo. 5s. net. [Very few remain.

ATTILA, MY ATTILA! A DRAMA IN FOUR ACTS.
With a Facsimile of Two Medals. (Uniform with
Stephania). Pott 4to. 5s. net.

"Attila, My Attila, is another of Michael Field's notable plays."—*Daily News.*
"Michael Field has already established a claim that what she writes should be
read."—*Times.*
"A poetic drama, it is, for a wonder, poetry, and framed on no archaic pattern;
its words speak to listeners of to-day."—*Album.*

GALTON (ARTHUR).

ESSAYS UPON MATTHEW ARNOLD.   [In preparation.

GASKIN (ARTHUR).

GOOD KING WENCESLAS. A Carol written by Dr. NEALE
and Pictured by ARTHUR J. GASKIN; with an Introduction by WILLIAM MORRIS. 4to. 3s. 6d. net.

Transferred to the present Publisher.

"Mr. Arthur J. Gaskin has more than redeemed the promise of his illustrations
to Hans Christian Andersen's tales by his edition of the late Dr. Neale's carol of
'Good King Wenceslas.' . . . . The pictures, pictorial borders, and initial letters
are remarkable both for the vigour of the drawing and the sense of the decorative
style which they exhibit. Mr. William Morris has shown his interest in the artist's
work by contributing a prefatory note."—*Daily News.*

GASKIN (MRS. ARTHUR).

DIVINE AND MORAL SONGS. By ISAAC WATTS, D.D. Pictured in Colours, by Mrs. ARTHUR GASKIN. 16mo. Printed by EDMUND EVANS. 3s. 6d. net.

A.B.C. An Alphabet Rhymed and Pictured by MRS. ARTHUR GASKIN. 60 designs. Fcap. 8vo. 3s. 6d. net. *Chicago : A. C. McClurg & Co.* [*Second thousand.*

" Quite an artistic book for children, the little rhymes to each letter are amusing and the woodcut elaboration of each are of the dear old-fashioned sort that are always so charming."—*Glasgow Herald.*

"Will delight children by its simple rhymes and the pretty and fanciful drawings which illustrate them. Mrs. Gaskin succeeds in rendering the essential grace of child-like life."—*Manchester Guardian.*

"The daintiest little book imaginable."—*Saturday Review.*

" This charming and dainty little volume will please most mothers, if not most children. The drawings are very clever, and full of the innocent humour and sweetness of childhood. Some of them are quite beautiful in their simple way, and the verses are in keeping with the pictures. . . . The volume is produced in excellent taste, and the binding is perfect in its way."—*Academy.*

HAKE (DR. T. GORDON, "The Parable Poet.")

MADELINE, AND OTHER POEMS. Crown 8vo. 5s. net.
Transferred to the present Publisher.

"The ministry of the angel Daphne to her erring human sister is frequently related in strains of pure and elevated tenderness. Nor does the poet who can show so much delicacy fail in strength. The description of Madeline as she passes in trance to her vengeance is full of vivid pictures and charged with tragic feeling.
The individuality of the writer lies in his deep sympathy with whatever affects the being and condition of man. . . . Taken as a whole, the book has high and unusual claims."—*Athenæum.*

"I have been reading 'Madeline' again. For sheer originality, both of conception and of treatment, I consider that it stands alone."—MR. THEODORE WATTS-DUNTON.

PARABLES AND TALES. (Mother and Child.—The Cripple.—The Blind Boy.—Old Morality.—Old Souls.—The Lily of the Valley.—The Deadly Nightshade.—The Poet). 9 illustrations by ARTHUR HUGHES. New Edition, with Memoir by THEODORE WATTS-DUNTON. [*In preparation.*

" The qualities of Dr. Gordon Hake's work were from the first fully admitted and warmly praised by one of the greatest of contemporary poets, who was also a critic of exceptional acuteness—Rossetti. Indeed, the only two review articles which Rossetti ever wrote were written on two of Dr. Hake's books: 'Madeline,' which he reviewed in the *Academy* in 1871, and 'Parables and Tales,' which he reviewed in the *Fortnightly* in 1873. Many eminent critics have expressed a decided preference for 'Parables and Tales' to Dr. Hake's other works, and it had the advantage of being enriched with the admirable illustrations of Arthur Hughes."—*Saturday Review,* January, 1895.

HAKE (DR. T. GORDON)—continued.

"'The piece called 'Old Souls' is probably secure of a distinct place in the literature of our day, and we believe the same may be predicted of other poems in the little collection just issued. . . . Should Dr. Hake's more restricted, but lovely and sincere contributions to the poetry of real life not find the immediate response they deserve, he may at least remember that others also have failed to meet at once with full justice and recognition. But we will hope for good encouragement to his present and future work; and can at least ensure the lover of poetry that in these simple pages he shall find not seldom a humanity limpid and pellucid—the well-spring of a true heart, with which his tears must mingle as with their own element.

"Dr. Hake has been fortunate in the beautiful drawings which Mr. Arthur Hughes has contributed to his little volume. No poet could have a more congenial yoke-fellow than this gifted aud imaginative artist."—D. G. ROSSETTI, in the *Fortnightly*. 1873.

HARTE (WALTER BLACKBURN).

MEDITATIONS IN MOTLEY: A Bundle of Papers imbued with the Sobriety of Midnight. Fcap. 8vo. 3s. 6d. net.

" . . . His style is good, because it so excellently conveys his thought. . . . At his best—that is in his most characteristic and seemingly unconscious passages—he reminds one of Montaigne, the charming inconsequence, the egotism free from arrogance."—*Academy*.

HAZLITT (W. CAREW).

THE LAMBS: THEIR LIVES, THEIR FRIENDS, AND THEIR CORRESPONDENTS. New Particulars and New Material. Thick crown 8vo.   6s. net.

This work contains (1) new biographical and bibliographical matter relative to Charles Lamb and his Sister; (2) sixty-four uncollected letters and notes from the Lambs, several of which have not hitherto been printed; and (3) certain letters to Lamb now first correctly rendered.

HEMINGWAY (PERCY).

THE HAPPY WANDERER (Poems). With title design by Charles I. ffoulkes. Printed at the CHISWICK PRESS, on hand-made paper. Sq. 16mo. 5s. net.

Chicago: Way & Williams.

"'The Happy Wanderer' is an exquisite volume where thought and expression alike are admirable. It should be read by all who are interested in the poetry of the day."—*Black and White*.

"Mr. Hemingway is thoughtful, and his felicity of phrase is more than occasional. His description of the sea as 'that mighty organ only God can play,' is very fine, and some of the sonnets—notably that which gives the title—linger in the memory and may not be forgotten."—*Review of Reviews*.

HEMINGWAY (PERCY)—continued.

" He has a touch of true poetic genius—quite enough to give throbbing life to nearly every stanza in this dainty little book. And with the strength and fervour there is grace. These are poems which all lovers of poetry will enjoy."—*Daily Mail.*

OUT OF EGYPT: Stories from the Threshold of the East. Cover design by GLEESON WHITE. Crown 8vo. 3s. 6d. *net.*

" This is a strong book."—*Academy.*

"The tale . . . is treated with daring directness. . . An impressive and pathetic close to a story told throughout with arresting strength and simplicity."—*Daily News.*

"Genuine power and pathos."—*Pall Mall Gazette.*

HICKEY (EMILY).

POEMS. With a Frontispiece by MARY E. SWAN. Crown 8vo. 5s. *net.*

" This book of true and pure poetry is brought out with that care and taste for which Mr. Elkin Mathews' publications are famous.'—*Irish Monthly.*

" It has charm and atmosphere, the grace of an exalted and truthful personality. . . . Phrases of her work which suggest how deeply she has pondered upon modern life ; seeing it steadily and whole, as a poet ought."—*Weekly Sun.*

" Miss Hickey's verse (in Lady Ellen) has a rich dignity of language and quaint beauty of phrase."—*Irish Times.*

VERSE TALES, LYRICS AND TRANSLATIONS. Printed at the ARNOLD PRESS. Imp. 16mo. 5s. *net.*
[*Very few remain.*

'Miss Hickey's ' Verse Tales, Lyrics, and Translations' almost invariably reach a high level of finish and completeness. The book is a string of little rounded pearls.—*Athenæum.*

HINKSON (HENRY A.).

DUBLIN VERSES. By MEMBERS OF TRINITY COLLEGE. Selected and Edited by H. A. HINKSON, late Scholar of Trinity College, Dublin. Pott 4to. 5s. *net.*

Dublin: Hodges, Figgis & Co., Limited.

Includes contributions by the following :—Aubrey de Vere, Sir Stephen de Vere, Oscar Wilde, J. K. Ingram, A. P. Graves, J. Todhunter, W. E. H. Lecky, T. W. Rolleston, Edward Dowden, G. A. Greene, Savage-Armstrong, Douglas Hyde, R. Y. Tyrrell, G. N. Plunkett, W. Macneile Dixon, William Wilkins, George Wilkins, and Edwin Hamilton.

" A pleasant volume of contemporary Irish Verse. . . A judicious selection."—*Times.*

" Wherever there is a group of Irish readers in near or far-off lands, these ' Dublin Verses' will be sure to command attention and applause."—*Glasgow Herald.*

HINKSON (*KATHARINE*).

A LOVER'S BREAST KNOT: Lyrics by KATHARINE TYNAN (MRS. HINKSON). Decorated title-page. Fcap. 8vo. 3s. 6d. *net*.

SLOES ON THE BLACKTHORN: A VOLUME OF IRISH STORIES. Crown 8vo., 3s. 6d. *net*. [*In preparation*.

"*HOBBY HORSE (THE)*."

AN ILLUSTRATED ART MISCELLANY. Edited by HERBERT P. HORNE. The Fourth Number of the New Series will shortly appear, after which MR. MATHEWS will publish all the numbers in a volume, price £1. 1s. *net*.

Boston: Copeland & Day.

HORNE (*HERBERT P.*)

DIVERSI COLORES: Poems. Vignette, &c., designed by the Author. Printed at the CHISWICK PRESS. 250 copies. 16mo. 5s. *net*.

Transferred by the Author to the present Publisher.

" In these few poems Mr. Horne has set before a tasteless age, and an extravagant age, examples of poetry which, without fear or hesitation, we consider to be of true and pure beauty."—*Anti-Jacobin*.

HOVEY (*RICHARD*).
See CARMAN.

HUGHES (*ARTHUR*).
See HAKE.

HUNT (*LEIGH*).

A VOLUME OF ESSAYS now collected for the first time. Edited with a critical Introduction by R. W. M. JOHNSON. [*In preparatoin*.

IMAGE (*SELWYN*).

POEMS AND CAROLS. (*Diversi Colores* Series.—New Volume). Title design by H. P. HORNE. Printed on hand-made paper at the CHISWICK PRESS. 16mo. 5s. *net*.

" Among the artists who have turned poets will shortly have to be reckoned Mr. Selwyn Image. A volume of poems from his pen will be published by Mr. Elkin Mathews before long. Those who are acquainted with Mr. Selwyn Image's work will expect to find a real and deep poetic charm in this book."—*Daily Chronicle*.

" No one else could have done it (*i.e.*, written 'Poems and Carols') in just this way, and the artist himself could have done it in no other way." " A remarkable

IMAGE (SELWYN)—continued.

impress of personality, and this personality of singular rarity and interest. Every piece is perfectly composed; the 'mental cartooning,' to use Rossetti's phrase, has been adequately done . . . an air of grave and homely order . . . a union of quaint and subtly simple homeliness, with a somewhat abstract severity. . . . It is a new thing, the revelation of a new poet. . . . Here is a book which may be trusted to outlive most contemporary literature."--*Saturday Review.*

"An intensely personal expression of a personality of singular charm, gravity, fancifulness, and interest; work which is alone among contemporary verse alike in regard to substance and to form . . . comes with more true novelty than any book of verse published in England for some years."—*Athenæum.*

"Some men seem to avoid fame as sedulously as the majority seek it. Mr. Selwyn Image is one of these. He has achieved a charming fame by his very shyness and mystery. His very name has a look of having been designed by the Century Guild, and it was certainly first published in *The Century Guild Hobby Horse*."—*The Realm.*

"In the tiny little volume of verse, 'Poems and Carols,' by Selwyn Image, we discern a note of spontaneous inspiration, a delicate and graceful fancy, and considerable, but unequal, skill of versification. The Carols are skilful reproductions of that rather archaic form of composition, devotional in tone and felicitous in sentiment. Love and nature are the principal themes of the Poems. It is difficult not to be hackneyed in the treatment of such themes, but Mr. Image successfully overcomes the difficulty."—*The Times.*

"The Catholic movement in literature, a strong reality to-day in England as in France, if working within narrow limits, has its newest interpretation in Mr. Selwyn Image's 'Poems and Carols.' Of course the book is charming to look at and to handle, since it is his. The Chiswick Press and Mr. Mathews have helped him to realize his design."—*The Sketch.*

ISHAM FACSIMILE REPRINTS; Nos. III. and IV.
See BRETON and SOUTHWELL.

*** New Elizabethan Literature at the British Museum, see *The Times*, 31 August, 1894, also *Notes and Queries*, Sept., 1894.

JOHNSON (LIONEL).

POEMS. With a title design and colophon by H. P. HORNE. Printed at the CHISWICK PRESS, on hand-made paper. Sq. post 8vo. 5s. *net.*

Also, 25 special copies at 15s. *net.*

Boston: Copeland and Day.

"Full of delicate fancy, and display much lyrical grace and felicity."—*Times.*

"An air of solidity, combined with something also of severity, is the first impression one receives from these pages. . . . The poems are more massive than most lyrics are; they aim at dignity and attain it. This is, we believe, the first book of verse that Mr. Johnson has published; and we would say, on a first reading, that for a first book it was remarkably mature. And so it is, in its accomplishment, its reserve of strength, its unfaltering style. . . . Whatever form his writing takes, it will be the expression of a rich mind, and a rare talent."—*Saturday Review.*

"Mr. Lionel Johnson's poems have the advantage of a two-fold inspiration. Many of these austere strains could never have been written if he had not been

JOHNSON (LIONEL)—continued.

steeped in the most golden poetry of the Greeks; while, on the other hand, side by
side with the mellifluous chanting, there comes another note, mild, sweet, and
unsophisticated—the very bird-note of Celtic poetry. And then again one comes on
a very ripe and affluent, as of one who has spoiled the very goldenest harvests of song
of cultivated ages. . . . Mr. Johnson's poetry is concerned with lofty things and
is never less than passionately sincere. It is sane, high-minded, and full of felicities."
—*Illustrated London News.*

"The most obvious characteristics of Mr. Johnson's verse are dignity and
distinction; but beneath these one feels a passionate poetic impulse, and a grave
fascinating music passes from end to end of the volume."—*Realm.*

"It is at once stately and passionate, austere, and free. His passion has a sane
mood: his fire a white heat. . . . Once again it is the Celtic spirit that makes
for higher things. Mr. Johnson's muse is concerned only with the highest. Her
flight is as of a winged thing, that goes 'higher still and higher,' and has few
flutterings near earth."—*Irish Daily Independent.*

JOHNSON (EFFIE).

IN THE FIRE, AND OTHER FANCIES. With frontispiece
by WALTER CRANE. Imperial 16mo. 3s. 6d. *net.*

KING (PAULINE).

ALIDA CRAIG: A Novel. With Illustrations by T. K.
HANNA. Thick fcap. 8vo. 3s. 6d. *net.*

LAMB (CHARLES).

BEAUTY AND THE BEAST. With an Introduction by
ANDREW LANG. Facsimile Reprint of the rare First
Edition. *With 8 choice stipple engravings in brown
ink, after the original plates.* Royal 16mo. 3s. 6d. *net.*
Transferred to the present Publisher.

See also HAZLITT.

LEGENDRE (ADAM),

THE LETTERS AND PAPERS OF. (*Diversi Colores* Series.)
[*In preparation.*

MARSON (REV. C. L.).

TURNPIKE TALES. With cover design by EDITH CALVERT.
Crown 8vo. 3s. 6d. *net.*

CONTENTS :—Mr. Lavender and his Legacy ; Wild Grapes ;
Miss Pattie's Rheumatism ; The Bishop ; A Realist of the Oldest
School ; Love in a Mist ; Abdias of Babylon ; A Satellite of
Saturn.

MARSTON (PHILIP BOURKE).

A LAST HARVEST: LYRICS AND SONNETS FROM THE BOOK OF LOVE. Edited, with Biographical Sketch, by LOUISE CHANDLER MOULTON. 500 copies. Printed by MILLER & SON. Post 8vo. 5s. net.

[*Very few remain.*

Also 50 copies on hand-made L.P. 10s. 6d. net.

[*Very few remain.*

"Among the sonnets with which the volume concludes, there are some fine examples of a form of verse in which all competent authorities allow that Marston excelled. 'The Breadth and Beauty of the Spacious Night,' 'To All in Haven,' 'Friendship and Love,' 'Love's Deserted Palace'—these, to mention no others, have the 'high seriousness' which Matthew Arnold made the test of true poetry."—*Athenæum.*

MASON (A. E. W.).

A ROMANCE OF WASTDALE. By the Author of "The Courtship of Morrice Buckler." Cr. 8vo. 3s. 6d. net. *New York: Frederick A. Stokes Company.*

"This story of few days is full of interest from first to last, culminating in so powerful a description of the tragic avenging of a double betrayal, that, as the ghastly events of the night in the mountain passes unfold themselves hour by hour, the excitement becomes intense. The book is full of events of an original and striking nature, and the characters sketched in by subtle, telling touches. We have rarely found a better told scene than that between Kate and Hawke, which the hidden bridegroom of the morrow sees and hears. The lovely lake land is described by one who knows and loves it. Few commencing 'A Romance of Wastdale' will lay it down till the last page is turned."—*Pall Mall Gazette.*

"Cleverly planned and brightly written."—*Black and White.*

"May be recommended for the grace of its style, as well as the interest of its plot."—*Daily Telegraph.*

MEYNELL (WILFRID).

THE CHILD SET IN THE MIDST. By MODERN POETS. With Introduction by W. MEYNELL, and Facsimile of the MS. of the "Toys" by COVENTRY PATMORE. Royal 16mo. 3s. 6d. net.

MORRIS (WILLIAM).

See GASKIN.

MORRISON (G. E.).

ALONZO QUIXANO, otherwise DON QUIXOTE: being a dramatization of the Novel of CERVANTES, and especially of those parts which he left unwritten. Cr. 8vo. 1s. net.

"This play, distinguished and full of fine qualities, is a brave attempt to enrich our poetic drama. . . . The reverence shown for Cervantes, the care to preserve intact the characteristics the Spanish master lingered over so humorously, yet so lovingly, have led Mr. Morrison to deserved and notable success."—*Academy.*

MUSA CATHOLICA.   [*In preparation.*

MURRAY (ALMA).

PORTRAIT AS BEATRICE CENCI. With Critical Notice
containing Four Letters from ROBERT BROWNING.
8vo. 2s. *net.*

NOEL (HON. RODEN).

MY SEA, and other posthumous Poems. With an Introduction by STANLEY ADDLESHAW. Cr. 8vo. 3s. 6d.
net.

" The volume now published from the materials the Hon. Roden Noel left behind
him will no way detract from his fame as a poet. We have here notes of the same
music that give so sweet and subtle a charm to his best poetry."—*Glasgow Herald.*
"The ' Nature Poems ' have lines of great beauty and vigour."—*Sketch.*
" Many of the poems in this slender volume are among the best, in our opinion,
that he ever wrote."—*Commonwealth.*
" A volume of strong and pathetic interest."—MR. A. E. FLETCHER, in the
New Age.
" Such poems as ' Wild Love on the Sea,' with its ringing rhythm and the tender
melodious ' To a Comrade,' leave little to be desired."—*Pall Mall Gazette.*

POOR PEOPLE'S CHRISTMAS. Printed at the AYLESBURY
PRESS. 250 copies. 16mo. 1s. *net.* [*Very few remain.*

"Displays the author at his best. . . . . Mr. Noel always has something
to say worth saying, and his technique—though like Browning, he is too intent upon
idea to bestow all due care upon form—is generally sufficient and sometimes
masterly. We hear too seldom from a poet of such deep and kindly sympathy."—
Sunday Times.

O'SULLIVAN (VINCENT).

POEMS. With a title design by SELWYN IMAGE. Printed
at the CHISWICK PRESS on hand-made paper. (Uniform
with LIONEL JOHNSON'S POEMS). Sq. cr. 8vo. 5s. *net.*

' These poems are of a rich, deep sweetness, that suits well the mystical devotion
of the faith that has inspired them. . . . Lovers of true poetry will do well to
spend a few quiet hours with Mr. O'Sullivan."—*Liverpool Mercury.*
"Very musical are his lullabies and croons—they go to the heart."—*Weekly
Register.*
"The soul of a bibliophilist will certainly be delighted by the sight of this
volume."—*Tablet.*

PHILLIPS (STEPHEN).

CHRIST IN HADES, and other POEMS (ELKIN MATHEWS'
SHILLING GARLAND, NO. III.).

[*Third Edition in the press.*

"It is a wonderful dream, a dream that stirs the heart in almost every line, though Christ himself never utters a word throughout the poem, but only brings his sad countenance and bleeding brow and torn hands into that imaginary world of half conceived and chaotic gloom."—*Spectator.*

"This much at least is certain, that here we have a new and powerful individuality, standing quite alone among our younger poets, and one who has the courage to attempt a sustained effort on a great theme. . . . We welcome this poem as a high performance seriously undertaken and powerfully carried through, and as deeply felt as it is vividly imagined."—*Saturday Review.*

"The solemn music is matched by majestic words. The poignancy of feeling which is in the title-poem cries from the lyrics also."—*Speaker.*

" . . . Mr. Phillips has made an essay and a splendidly successful essay towards the epic. . . . It deals with a single episode in Christian legend, and one feels admiration for a writer who has selected for his theme so lofty a subject, adorned it with such majestic music, and created for it such a striking atmosphere of solemnity and gloom. . . . There is something Miltonic in the massive dignity of the lines. . . . 'Christ in Hades' is a fine imaginative poem of a rare order, which everyone ought to read."—*Echo.*

POWELL (F. YORK).

See CORBIN.

PROBYN (MAY).

PANSIES : A BOOK OF POEMS. With a title-page and cover design by MINNIE MATHEWS. Fcap. 8vo. 3s. 6d. net.

"Miss Probyn's new volume is a slim one, but rare in quality. She is no mere pretty verse maker; her spontaneity and originality are beyond question, and so far as colour and picturesqueness go, only Mr. Francis Thompson rivals her among the English Catholic poets of to-day."—*Sketch.*

"This too small book is a mine of the purest poetry, very holy, and very refined, and removed as far as possible from the tawdry or the common-place."—*Irish Monthly.*

"The religious poems are in their way perfect, with a tinge of the mysticism one looks for in the poetry of two centuries ago, but so seldom meets with nowadays."—*Catholic Times.*

" Full of a delicate devotional sentiment and much metrical felicity."—*Times.*

New Illustrated Edition of a scarce book.

RADFORD (DOLLIE).

A LIGHT LOAD : a Book of Songs. With numerous full-page drawings and initial letters by BEATRICE PARSONS. Small 8vo. 5s. net.

RADFORD (DOLLIE)—*continued.*

"No woman could write a sweeter verse than the dedicatory stanzas of Dollie Radford's 'A Light Load.'"—*Speaker.*

"Of one piece, it should be said that it breathes the spirit of Mr. R. L. Stevenson's 'A Child's Garden of Verses.' Indeed there is not a song in this slender volume that would not bear quoting as an example of what a lyric should be."—*Daily Chronicle.*

"The songs are full of instinctive music which soars naturally. They have the choice unsought felicity of a nature essentially lyrical."—*Academy.*

"There is a song to quote on every page, and we must desist, but we are much mistaken if Mrs. Radford is not the possessor os a very rare and exquisite lyric gift indeed."—MR. RICHARD LE GALLIENNE, in the *Star.*

RHYMERS' CLUB, THE SECOND BOOK OF THE.

Contributions by E. DOWSON, E. J. ELLIS, G. A. GREENE, A. HILLIER, LIONEL JOHNSON, RICHARD LE GALLIENNE, VICTOR PLARR, E. RADFORD, E. RHYS, T. W. ROLLESTONE, ARTHUR SYMONS, J. TODHUNTER, W. B. YEATS. Printed by MILLER & SON. 500 copies (of which 400 are for sale). 16mo. 5*s. net.*
·   50 copies on hand-made L.P.   10*s. 6d. net.*

New York: Dodd, Mead & Co.

"The work of twelve very competent verse writers, many of them not unknown to fame. This form of publication is not a new departure exactly, but it is a recurrence to the excellent fashion of the Elizabethan age, when 'England's Helicon,' Davison's 'Poetical Rhapsody,' and 'Phœnix Nest,' with scores of other collections, contained the best songs of the best song-writers of that tuneful epoch."—*Black and White.*

"The future of these thirteen writers, who have thus banded themselves together, will be watched with interest. Already there is fulfilment in their work, and there is much promise."—*Speaker.*

"In the intervals of Welsh rarebit and stout provided for them at the 'Cheshire Cheese,' in Fleet Street, the members of the Rhymers' Club have produced some very pretty poems, which Mr. Elkin Mathews has issued in his notoriously dainty manner."—*Pall Mall Gazette.*

ROSEN (LEW).

NAPOLEON'S OPERA - GLASS : A HISTRIONIC STUDY. With a cover design by EDITH CALVERT. Crown 8vo. 3*s. 6d. net.*

This monograph treats of Napoleon as a critic and patron of the drama, and touches upon his relations with playwrights and players.

RUDING (WALTER).

AN EVIL MOTHERHOOD. An Impressionist Novel. With a Frontispiece by AUBREY BEARDSLEY. Crown 8vo. 3s. 6d. net.

"The story is, indeed, a powerful one; a tale of wrong and suffering told in a vivid and thrilling language. It is in very truth the tragedy of a brain—its revolt, its suffering, its final passionate cries against the cruel wrong which sapped its strength, tortured its intellect and intelligence, and then left it thus shattered to fight the healthy world as best it could."—*Sunday Times.*

"Extremely original in its treatment."—*Westminster Gazette.*

SCHAFF (DR. PHILLIP).

DANTE PAPERS. With Illustrations by W. T. HORTON.
[*In preparation.*

LITERATURE AND POETRY. Engravings. 8vo. 10s. net.

SCULL (W. DELAPLAINE).

THE GARDEN OF THE MATCHBOXES, and other Stories. Crown 8vo. 3s. 6d. net.

"The author of these clever and fascinating fantasies is entirely abreast of the newest critical orthodoxy. . . . As literary craftsmanship, these maiden stories attain an unusually high and even level. They are all style. The variety of subject and motive is remarkable. As a whole, I take it, these tales mark the advent of a new story-teller, adequately equipped for the delineation of character, and possessed of acute psychological insight. Besides which, he can write.'—MR. GRANT ALLEN, in *Academy.*

"The beauty and pathos of 'A Certain Mr. Smith' will reward everyone for taking up the book."—*Manchester Guardian.*

"It is some time since we came upon more original work than this."—*Illustrated London News.*

SHARP (WILLIAM).

ECCE PUELLA, AND OTHER PROSE IMAGININGS. Cr. 8vo. 3s. 6d. net.

"The book, as a whole, will appeal to all who have a keen palate for the more subtle flavours of literature."—*New Age.*

"Written in Mr. Sharp's brightest and happiest style."—*Leeds Mercury.*

SHILLING GARLAND (ELKIN MATHEWS').

Price One Shilling, net, each part.

No. I. LONDON VISIONS. By L. BINYON.
[*Second Edition.*

No. II. PURCELL ODE. By R. BRIDGES.
[*Second Edition.*

SHILLING GARLAND (ELKIN MATHEWS')—continued.

No. III.   CHRIST IN HADES.   By S. PHILLIPS.
[Third Edition in press.

No. IV.   AEROMANCY.   By M. L. WOODS.
[Second Edition in press.

No. V.   SONGS AND ODES.   By CANON DIXON.
[Just ready.

No. VI.   THE PRAISE OF LIFE.   By L. BINYON.
[In preparation.

No. VII.   NEW POEMS.   By STEPHEN PHILLIPS.
[In preparation.

** Other Volumes in preparation.

The first five parts may also be had bound in cloth, 5s. 6d. net.

SONG OF SONGS, WHICH IS SOLOMON'S.

Twenty Drawings from designs by ALTHEA GYLES.   4to.
One Guinea *net.*

Also 25 copies on special paper, Two Guineas *net.*
[In preparation.
[Isham Facsimile Reprint].

S[OUTHWELL] (R[OBERT]).

A FOVREFOVLD MEDITATION, OF THE FOURE LAST
THINGS.   COMPOSED IN A DIUINE POEME.   By R. S.
The author of S. Peter's complaint.   London, 1606.
A Facsimile Reprint, with a Bibliographical Note by
CHARLES EDMONDS.   150 copies.   Printed on hand-
made paper at the CHISWICK PRESS.   Roy. 16mo.
5s. *net.*

Also 50 copies, large paper.   7s. 6d. *net.*

Facsimile reprint from the unique fragment discovered in the autumn of 1867 by
Mr. Charles Edmonds in a disused lumber room at Lamport Hall, Northants, and
lately purchased by the British Museum authorities.   This fragment supplies the first
sheet of a previously unknown poem by Robert Southwell, the Roman Catholic poet,
whose religious fervour lends a pathetic beauty to everything that he wrote, and
future editors of Southwell's works will find it necessary to give it close study.   The
whole of the Poem has been completed from two MS. copies, which differ in the
number of Stanzas.

SPANISH ARMADA.

A LETTER written on October 4, 1589, by Captain Cuellar, of the Spanish Armada, to H.M. King Philip II., recounting his Misadventures in Ireland and elsewhere after the Wreck of his Ship.   Translated with Notes, by HENRY D. SEDGWICK.   Finely printed on deckle-edge paper.   250 copies only.   Fcap. 8vo.   4s. 6d. net.

Translated from the Spanish text given in Captain Fernandez Duro's *La Armada Invincible*. The letter is of extreme interest, and gives a graphic picture of the demoralization of the Armada as it made its final attempt to circumnavigate Scotland and Ireland, and of the sufferings of the multitudes who were wrecked on the Irish coast. Cuellor was wrecked in O'Rourke's country, and with many romantic adventures made his way to that of O'Cahan, where he finally found ship for Scotland. His picture of the condition of Ireland is sufficiently horrible. Altogether an extraordinary account of Ireland and her 'Savages.'

SYMONDS (JOHN ADDINGTON).

IN THE KEY OF BLUE, AND OTHER PROSE ESSAYS. With cover designed by C. S. RICKETTS.   Printed at the BALLANTYNE PRESS.   Third Edition.   Thick cr. 8vo.   8s. 6d. net.

New York: Macmillan & Co.

"The variety of Mr. Symonds' interests! Here are criticisms upon the Venetian Tiepolo, upon M. Zola, upon Mediæval Norman Songs, upon Elizabethan lyrics, upon Plato's and Dante's ideals of love; and not a sign anywhere, except may be in the last, that he has more concern for, or knowledge of, one theme than another. Add to these artistic themes the delightful records of English or Italian scenes, with their rich beauties of nature or of art, and the human passions that inform them. How joyous a sense of great possessions won at no man's hurt or loss must such a man retain."—*Daily Chronicle.*

"Some of the essays are very charming, in Mr. Symonds' best style, but the first one, that which gives its name to the volume, is at least the most curious of the lot."—*Speaker.*

"The other essays are the work of a sound and sensible critic."—*National Observer.*

"The literary essays are more restrained, and the prepared student will find them full of illumination and charm, while the descriptive papers have the attractiveness which Mr. Symonds always gives to work in this *genre*."—MR. JAS. ASHCROFT NOBLE, in *The Literary World.*

TENNYSON (LORD).

See HALLAM,—VAN DYKE.

TYNAN (KATHARINE).

See HINKSON.

VAN DYKE (HENRY).

THE POETRY OF TENNYSON.   Fifth Edition, enlarged.
Cr. 8vo.   5s. 6d. net.

*The additions consist of a Portrait, Two Chapters, and the
Bibliography expanded.   The Laureate himself gave valuable
aid in correcting various details.*

"Mr. Elkin Mathews publishes a new edition, revised and enlarged, of that
excellent work, 'The Poetry of Tennyson,' by Henry Van Dyke. The additions
are considerable. It is extremely interesting to go over the bibliographical notes
to see the contemptuous or, at best, contemptuously patronising tone of the reviewers
in the early thirties gradually turning to civility, to a loud chorus of applause."—
Anti-Jacobin.

"Considered as an aid to the study of the Laureate, this labour of love merits
warm commendation. Its grouping of the poems, its bibliography and chronology,
its catalogue of Biblical allusion and quotations, are each and all substantial accessories
to the knowledge of the author."—DR. RICHARD GARNETT, in the *Illustrated
London News.*

"As an antidote to Mr. Churton Collins on Tennyson, Mr. Elkin Mathews sends
a new edition of Dr. Van Dyke's admirable exposition of the poet, 'The Poetry of
Tennyson.'"—MR. RICHARD LE GALLIENNE, in the *Star.*

WALKER (JOHN).
SPANISH IDYLLS.   [*In preparation.*

WATSON (E. H. LACON).

THE UNCONSCIOUS HUMOURIST, AND OTHER ESSAYS.
Second Edition.   Crown 8vo.   4s. 6d. net.
New York: George H. Richmond & Co.

"It is the best book of desultory essays given to us since the unapproachable
master of this form was carried to his long rest on Vailima height. . . .   He
touches on many subjects deftly. A note of pathos, a sly stroke of humour, a sug-
gestion of philosophy deep enough to tickle one into momentary activity of thought,
are his devices. The result is pleasing entertainment, and a storing away in the
memory of not a few ingenious and happily inspired phrases. . . ."—PERCY
ADDLESHAW, in the *Academy.*

"Very readable essays—humorous, superficial, contemplative: you may call
them all these things—on a variety of subjects, from love to bicycle tours."—*Bookman.*

"These papers display a high and well-maintained standard of literary capacity,
together with a robust development of the critical faculty. . . .   The remaining
essays, while keenly introspective, are, like those more particularly referred to above,
agreeably free from the cheap cynicism that characterises so many modern productions
of this class. Eminently readable are the papers headed 'Bicycle Tours,' 'An Exami-
nation of the Commonplace,' 'Prophers of the Mist,' 'The Waters of Castaly,' and
'Cacoethes Scribendi,' in all of which amusement is felicitously combined with
instruction."—*Daily Telegraph.*

"A pleasantly written and readable volume of essays. . . ."—*Scotsman.*

"Mr. Watson's nice and well-printed little collection of essays will prove a
pleasant companion on some of these bicycle tours, whose praises he sings so well.
. . . ."—*Glasgow Herald.*

[Mr. Wedmore's Short Stories.   New and Uniform Issue. Crown 8vo., each Volume 3s. 6d. net.]

WEDMORE (FREDERICK).

PASTORALS OF FRANCE. Fourth Edition. Crown 8vo.
3s. 6d. net.   [*Ready.*
New York: Charles Scribner's Sons.

"A writer in whom delicacy of literary touch is united with an almost disembodied fineness of sentiment."—*Athenæum*.

"Of singular quaintness and beauty."—*Contemporary Review*.

RENUNCIATIONS. Third Edition. With a Portrait by
J. J. SHANNON. Cr. 8vo. 3s. 6d. net.   [*Ready.*
New York: Charles Scribner's Sons.

"These are clever studies in polite realism."—*Athenæum*.

"They are quite unusual. The picture of Richard Pelse, with his one moment of romance, is exquisite."—*St. James's Gazette*.

"'The Chemist in the Suburbs,' in 'Renunciations,' is a pure joy. . . . The story of Richard Pelse's life is told with a power not unworthy of the now disabled hand that drew for us the lonely old age of M. Parent."—MR. TRAILL, in *The New Review*.

"The book belongs to the highest order of imaginative work. 'Renunciations' are studies from the life—pictures which make plain to us some of the innermost workings of the heart."—*Academy*.

"Mr. Wedmore has gained for himself an enviable reputation. His style has distinction, has form. He has the poet's secret how to bring out the beauty of common things. . . 'The Chemist in the Suburbs,' in 'Renunciations,' is his masterpiece."—*Saturday Review*.

ENGLISH EPISODES. Second Edition. Cr. 8vo. 3s. 6d.
net.   [*Ready.*
New York: Charles Scribner's Sons.

"Distinction is the characteristic of Mr. Wedmore's manner. These things remain on the mind as things seen ; not read of."—*Daily News*.

"A penetrating insight, a fine pathos. Mr. Wedmore is a peculiarly fine and sane and carefully deliberate artist."—*Westminster Gazette*.

There may also be had the Collected Edition (1893) of "Pastorals of France" and "Renunciations," with Title-page by John Fulleylove, R.I. 5s. net.

WICKSTEED (P. H., Warden of University Hall).

DANTE : SIX SERMONS.

** A FOURTH EDITION. (Unaltered Reprint). Cr. 8vo.
2s. net.

"It is impossible not to be struck with the reality and earnestness with which Mr. Wicksteed seeks to do justice to what are the supreme elements of the *Commedia*, its spiritual significance, and the depth and insight of its moral teaching."—*Guardian*.

WINSER (LILIAN).

LAYS AND LEGENDS OF THE WEALD OF KENT, AS SUNG AND RECOUNTED AT A TWELFTH-NIGHT PARTY. With Illustrations by MARGARET WINSER. Crown 8vo. 5s. net.

"In this volume a new writer introduces us to a land almost unknown in the realms of poesy, a region of fertile Kent, which has retained many of the characteristics of old times. An episode of rural courtship gives the contents a connected interest. The illustrations are conceived in the same spirit as the text. In Miss Winser's volume the yeoman and peasant of the pleasant southern county have found an exponent."

WOODS (MARGARET L.).

AËROMANCY AND OTHER POEMS. (ELKIN MATHEWS' SHILLING GARLAND, No. IV.).
[Second Edition in press.

"Mrs. Woods is a poet of great power and originality."—Globe.

"'Aëromancy' is a fine poem, but there are others in the slim volume likely to be more popular; 'The Mariner s Sleep by the Sea,' for instance, and still more so, 'The Child Alone'—the latter a delightful picture of an imaginative child."—Sketch.

"It ['Aëromancy'] contains some very beautiful verses, but to the uninitiated reader they are somewhat incoherent. . . . The gems of the small selection are—'An April Song' and 'The Child Alone.' The former is the very life and breath of April at its best. . . . The latter is an exquisite sketch. . . . It would be impossible to express the elaborate and buoyant make-believe of an imaginative child's reverie with more force and humour than are given in these spirited verses."—Spectator.

WYNNE (FRANCES).

WHISPER! A Volume of Verse. Fcap. 8vo. buckram. 2s. 6d. net.

Transferred by the Author to the present Publisher.

"A little volume of singularly sweet and graceful poems, hardly one of which can be read by any lover of poetry without definite pleasure, and everyone who reads either of them without is, we venture to say, unable to appreciate that play of light and shadow on the heart of man which is of the very essence of poetry."—Spectator.

"The book includes, to my humble taste, many very charming pieces, musical, simple, straightforward and not 'as sad as night.' It is long since I have read a more agreeable volume of verse, successful up to the measure of its aims and ambitions."—MR. ANDREW LANG, in Longman's Magazine.

YEATS (W. B.).

THE WIND AMONG THE REEDS (Poems). With a Cover Design by Althea Gyles. [In the press.

THE SHADOWY WATERS. A Poetic Play. [In preparation.

LONDON: VIGO STREET, W.

www.ingramcontent.com/pod-product-compliance
Lightning Source LLC
Chambersburg PA
CBHW032354020726
47499CB00008B/2749